Jemma's Journey

Jemma's Journey

by Trevor Romain

Illustrated by Pat Lopez

Boyds Mills Press

This story is inspired by the tragic events that took place in Ocoee, Florida, on November 2, 1920, after July Perry and Mose Norman, two African American men, were denied the right to vote. Though many details have been obscured by time, history records that violence erupted, which resulted in the burning of black homes and churches, and the loss of many lives.

Text copyright © 2002 by Trevor Romain
Illustrations copyright © 2002 by Pat Lopez

Published by Caroline House
Boyds Mills Press, Inc.
A Highlights Company
815 Church Street
Honesdale, Pennsylvania 18431
Printed in China

Publisher Cataloging-in-Publication Data

Romain, Trevor.
    Jemma's journey / by Trevor Romain : illustrated by Pat Lopez. —1st ed.
[32] p. : col. ill. ;   cm.
Summary: Jemma plants a tree in honor of a man who was hanged there in the 1920s.
ISBN 1-56397-937-3
1. African Americans—Suffrage—Florida—History—20th century—Juvenile
fiction. 2. Massacres—Ocoee—Florida—Fiction—Juvenile literature.
(1. African Americans—Suffrage—Florida—History—20th century—Fiction.
2. Massacres—Ocoee—Florida—Fiction.) I. Lopez, Pat. II. Title.
   [E] 21   2002   CIP
2001093642

First edition, 2002
The text of this book is set in 15-point Palatino.
Visit our Web site at www.boydsmillspress.com

10 9 8 7 6 5 4 3 2 1

In memory of my grandmother Sonia, whose own horrific journey as a child refugee led to the freedom I enjoy today

— T. R.

In memory of my nephew Ryan, whose wonderful life was tragically cut short

— P. L.

IT WAS A NIGHT OF RAIN and thunder and lazy talking around the kitchen table.

Everyone was bursting full from Grandma's pie. Mom and Dad and Grandma were talking, talking, talking. Jemma was looking through an old photo album, and Grandpa was snoring on the couch.

The talk at the table was about the old days and the pictures in the album. Grandma was going on about a town called Ocoee. A town where peaceful black folk like her sat under the camphor trees and jawed about the lives of the people who lived there.

She was remembering how everything
seemed fine in Ocoee until that day in November of
1920. The second of November it was. The date when
two black men tried to vote on election day.

Grandma was saying how the men were chased
away all because they wanted to vote.

How guns were raised and bullets flew. And how
the next morning many people lay dead.

"A day I will always remember to never forget," said Grandma. " 'Specially the dead man who was hanging from that tree. I'll never forget that."

Jemma thought how sad the man's family must have felt when they discovered him in the tree. Jemma had a feeling that no flowers ever grew under that tree again.

Grandma told how some men had cut that tree down because they didn't want to remember what happened.

"They should have left that tree," said Grandma. "It would have been a good memorial."

For a while the whole house was quiet. Even Grandpa stopped snoring. And Grandma, who had no teeth, chewed and chewed on her gums for a long while.
Then everyone went to bed.
Jemma tossed and turned all night in a worried sleep.

In the morning, the sun's warm arms
reached through the window to comfort
her, but Jemma was already long gone.
She rode her bicycle into town and
found Mr. Fervis at the nursery.

Jemma used her Christmas jar money and bought a small oak tree. It reached up to only her knees, but in her mind it was as big as her dreams.

She left her bicycle at the nursery and walked across the square to the bus station.

FERVIS
NURSERY

Jemma was happy when the smiling man in the ticket office didn't charge her extra for taking the tree on the bus.

"Make sure you plant that tree deep in the ground," he said. "That way the roots will grow strong. Like a growing family, a tree needs good strong roots to stand tall against all the wind and rain and thunder."

Jemma nodded.

She sat with the tree on her lap and gazed out the window as the wheels slowly dragged the big Greyhound bus out of town.

The bus vibrated with a numbing hum as it traveled along the country roads.

Some people got on the bus at the next stop. An old lady sat next to Jemma.

"That's a fine tree you have there," she said. "It has a good, solid trunk, it seems."

Jemma held the tree proudly.

The lady reached over and gently ran her tired crooked finger down the tree's little trunk. "Like people need solid beliefs to hang their lives onto, a tree needs a good, solid trunk to anchor all those little branches while they grow," she said softly.

"I think you're right," said Jemma.

A man sitting behind Jemma leaned forward and rested his chin on the seat back. "You know," he said, "when my daddy was on his way to dying, he told me a tree is but the nearest thing to life itself. He said all the leaves are like people. A healthy leaf needs a strong branch attached to a solid trunk, which is firmly held in the ground by its powerful roots."

Before Jemma could reply, the bus suddenly screeched to a stop, and the tree almost fell off her lap.

The front door hissed open, and a police officer got on the bus. He walked directly down the aisle and stopped next to Jemma.

"Jemma L. Williams?"

She nodded.

"Let's go," he said.

"But . . ."

"No buts," he replied. "I've got criminals to catch, and I hate wasting my time chasing ridiculous runaways like you."

"I'm not running away," mumbled Jemma as the officer propelled her forward by the scruff of her neck.

The police officer strapped Jemma and her tree into the front seat and got into the car. "I can't believe how crazy kids are these days," he said as they pulled away from the bus. "Why did you do something like that?"

So Jemma told him. She told him about Ocoee. She told him about that day in 1920 when decent people were killed just because they wanted to vote. She told him about the man hanging in the tree and how the tree was quickly cut down and forgotten.

"I feel sad because my grandmother is dying," Jemma told the police officer. "When she dies, some of the history she remembers will die, too."

Jemma shrugged, looking down at the tree. "I thought this tree would be a good way to keep my grandmother, and her memories of one important day, alive for a long time."

The police officer did not say anything for a while. Then he pulled over and turned the car around. They traveled the twenty-three miles to Ocoee in silence.

They drove around Ocoee until Jemma found the perfect place for the tree. The officer dug a hole, and together they put the tree in the ground and patted the soil. Jemma tied a note to the trunk.

After cleaning up, the officer gently placed his hand on Jemma's shoulder, and they walked back to the patrol car in silence.

Jemma glanced over her shoulder at the tree. The little white note attached to the trunk flapped comfortably in the wind.

The note said,

"Always remember to never forget."